This Topsy and Tim book belongs to

Published by Ladybird Books Ltd
80 Strand London WC2R ORL
A Penguin Company

5 7 9 10 8 6

© Jean and Gareth Adamson MCMXCVII, This edition MMV

The moral rights of the author/illustrator have been asserted
LADYBIRD and the device of a ladybird are trademarks of Ladybird Books Ltd
All rights reserved. No part of this publication may be reproduced, stored in a retrieval system,
or transmitted in any form or by any means, electronic, mechanical, photocopying, recording or otherwise,
without the prior consent of the copyright owner.

ISBN: 978-1-84422-635-1

Printed in China

Buckets and Spades

Jean and **Gareth Adamson**

Early one morning, Dad called, "Come along, tiddlers! We're ready to start."

Topsy and Tim ran to the car carrying their buckets and spades. They were going for a holiday at the seaside.

First they drove to the garage to get the car ready for the journey. The garage man put the petrol in while Dad blew up the tyres.

"The windscreen could do with a wash," said Mummy.

Topsy and Tim fetched the water in their seaside buckets.

"All aboard," shouted Dad.

Tim waved to the garage man as they drove away.

"Goodbye everybody!" called Topsy.
"We're going to the seaside."

They buzzed along until the town was far behind. Then they had to slow right down behind a big, smelly lorry.

Suddenly Tim shouted, "We've left our buckets behind!"

"Never mind," said Mummy. "We'll buy new buckets when we get there."

Tim began to cry. "I want my old bucket," he sobbed.

"We're all getting hungry," said
Mummy. "Let's stop and have
a picnic."

Dad drove down a narrow country lane
and pulled up by a farm gate. "Here's
a good place for a picnic," he said.

Soon it was time to go.

"We must pick up all our litter," said Mummy.

"What shall we put it in?" asked Tim.

Mummy gave them an empty carrier bag for the litter.

"We could have put it in our good old seaside buckets," said Topsy.

Dad began to turn the car round. Suddenly the back dropped down with a bump.

"We've gone into the ditch," said Dad.

Dad looked worried. "We need help," he said, "and here we are, miles from anywhere."

"I can hear a car," said Topsy.

The sound came nearer and stopped. Then a man looked over the hedge high above them.

"It's a friendly giant!" shouted Topsy and Tim.

The man wasn't a giant. He was sitting up in his tractor in the field behind the hedge. But he was friendly. He fixed a rope from his tractor to their car. Then the tractor tugged the car out of the ditch.

They drove on and soon came to the top of a hill.

"I can see the sea!" shouted Topsy.

"I wish we had our old buckets," said Tim.

Soon they reached their holiday village.
Dad began to unload their luggage.

"Hello!" he said. "What have I found?"

"Our buckets!" shouted Topsy and Tim.

They ran straight off to fill them
with seaside sand.

Match the colours.

Match the pairs.

How many buckets can you see?
How many seagulls?
How many boats?
How many children?

Tell the story.